MILK AND COOKIES

• FRANK ASCH •

ALADDIN
New York London Toronto Sydney New Delhi

ALADDIN

An imprint of Simon & Schuster Children's Publishing Division

1230 Avenue of the Americas, New York, NY 10020

This Aladdin edition March 2015

For information about special discounts for bulk purchases,
please contact Simon & Schuster Special Sales at 1-866-506-1949
or business@simonandschuster.com.

The Simon & Schuster Speakers Bureau can bring authors to your live event.
For more information or to book an event contact the
Simon & Schuster Speakers Bureau at 1-866-248-3049
or visit our website at www.simonspeakers.com.

Designed by Karina Granda

The text of this book was set in Olympian LT Std.

Printed in the United States of America 0315 LAK

2 4 6 8 10 9 7 5 3

Library of Congress Control Number 82-7962

ISBN 978-1-4424-6672-2 (hc)

ISBN 978-1-4424-6673-9 (pbk)

ISBN 978-1-4424-6674-6 (eBook)

To my uncles,
who love their woodstoves.

One winter day, the Bear family
went to visit Grandma and Grandpa.

When it got to be late,
too late to go home . . .

Grandma made up the couch
for them in the living room.

"Good night," said Grandma and Grandpa.

"Good night," said Mama and Papa.

"Good night," said Baby Bear.

And they all went to sleep.

In the middle of the night, Baby Bear heard a noise and woke up. Then he saw a strange red light coming from under the cellar door.

He climbed out of bed and tiptoed to the door to see what it was.

He didn't want to make any noise, so he just peeked through the keyhole.

What he saw looked like a giant dragon with flames shooting from its mouth. Grandpa was there feeding it.

When the dragon shut its mouth, Grandpa came upstairs.

"Is there anything wrong?" asked Grandpa.

"No, I'm okay," said Baby Bear.

"Would you like some milk and cookies?" asked Grandpa.

"No, thank you," said Baby Bear. And he went back to bed.

That night, Baby Bear dreamed
that the cellar door opened,

and the dragon . . .

came upstairs!

"I'm hungry," said the dragon.

Baby Bear ran into the kitchen,

and opened the refrigerator.

He poured the dragon a glass of milk

and opened a box of cookies.

"Thank you," said the dragon.

"I like milk and cookies."

And he ate everything all up.

He didn't save any milk or even one cookie for Baby Bear.

Just then, Baby Bear woke up crying.

Mama and Papa Bear woke up too.

Baby Bear told them his dream.

"Whatever gave you the idea that there was a dragon in the cellar?" asked Mama Bear.

"I saw it!" said Baby Bear.

"If I come downstairs with you,"
asked Papa Bear, "will you show
me the dragon?"
  "Okay," said Baby Bear.
  And they went downstairs.

In the corner where Baby Bear
thought he had seen a dragon,

there was a woodstove.

Papa Bear opened the door.

Inside, the flames glowed brightly.

"There, you see," said Papa Bear.
"There is no dragon in the cellar,
just an old woodstove."

When they went back upstairs, Grandma
and Grandpa were up.

"Is everything all right?" asked Grandma.

"It is now," said Papa Bear.

"Good!" said Grandpa.

"Let's all have some . . .

milk and cookies!"